A Thanksgiving Turkey

BY JULIAN SCHEER

ILLUSTRATED BY

RONALD HIMLER

Holiday House / *New York*

For Adrienne, Noah, Ginny, and Rich—my grandchildren
J. S.
For Ashlyn Rae and Preston James
R. H.

Text copyright © 2001 by Julian Scheer
Illustrations copyright © 2001 by Ronald Himler
All Rights Reserved
Printed in the United States of America
www.holidayhouse.com
First Edition
Library of Congress Cataloging-in-Publication Data
Scheer, Julian.
A Thanksgiving turkey / by Julian Scheer;
illustrated by Ronald Himler.—1st ed.
p. cm.
Summary: A thirteen-year-old boy and his mother move to a farm
in rural Virginia, where he and his grandfather try to hunt a wild turkey.
ISBN 0-8234-1674-7 (hardcover)
[1. Grandfathers—Fiction. 2. Wild turkey—Fiction. 3. Hunting—Fiction.
4. Thanksgiving Day—Fiction. 5. Farm life—Virginia—Fiction. 6. Virginia—Fiction.]
I. Himler, Ronald, ill. II. Title
PZ7.S3424 Th 2001   2001016644
[Fic]—dc21

I WAS THIRTEEN YEARS OLD when my mother and I moved to rural Virginia to live with my grandfather on his farm. He was "getting up in years," as my mother put it, and she thought it a good idea to be there to help him and, at the same time, she thought a farm would be a good place for a young boy to grow up.

I liked my school and my friends and the thought of leaving where we lived did not go over so well, but I had to make the most of it.

It was a small farm. Granddad planted a few acres of corn and he had another field where he made hay. He had a few steers, some pigs, a lot of chickens, a milk cow, along with a half dozen barn cats, and three or four hounds that followed him everywhere.

I soon fell into a routine. At daylight our farm became busy. Each of us had our chores to do. I fed the steers, chickens, and pigs. Mother fixed breakfast. Granddad brought in a pail of milk. After breakfast I walked to the end of our lane to catch the school bus.

As soon as spring arrived and the days grew longer, I began to like the farm more and more. Mother talked of the garden she would plant. Granddad promised to plant a row of sunflowers for her. And I looked forward to coming home to see what was going on.

On Saturdays and Sundays we took long walks and Granddad showed me animal tracks. Soon I could identify foxes, raccoons, and possums. Deer were easy to spot. Granddad showed me where turkeys had scratched for acorns and other nuts.

Granddad loved to talk about hunting turkeys. There was no skill, he said, in hunting deer or quail, especially when one used dogs. But hunting a wild turkey was something else, a test of wills. The wild turkey was, Granddad told me over and over again, the smartest, most clever, trickiest thing in the woods. One day, he promised, we'd go together and get a turkey. I began to dream of such a day.

It was on a Saturday in early April that I went on my first hunt for a wild turkey.

Granddad awakened me at four o'clock. I knew there would be a chill in the air, and I put on a sweater and a heavy jacket. When I reached the kitchen, Granddad took a coffeepot off the stove, trying not to wake my mother.

"Here," he said. "Try this."

"But I don't drink coffee," I told him.

"You'll need it today," he said, and I drank as much bitter coffee as I could.

I had never been outside that early. The moon was still bright, outlining the sheds and the barn. In the distance an owl hooted. Without a word I followed my grandfather down the path next to the plowed garden, through the back gate. We started across what would soon be a cornfield, alone in the silence of the morning. Occasionally a bird would fly up from a nest on the ground, sending chills down my spine.

After a while we were on the bank of Cedar Run. Granddad motioned for me to follow a bit to the right. A few feet away the bank gave way to a deep, soft path to the shoreline, a path carved from the bank by cattle that had come here for years to drink. We waded across a shallow spot, climbed the bank on the other side, and set out along an old logging trail.

By now the woods were beginning to come alive. Squirrels rushed from tree to ground, a red fox barked once and ran deeper into the woods, and the glow in the east told us the sun would soon break over the horizon. Granddad kept walking, saying nothing, and I followed as best I could. Finally we stopped and he sat on the ground, his back to a large fallen tree, his gun across his lap.

Granddad pulled out his caller. There are different callers.

His was a handmade pine box, and he pulled a piece of polished pine across its open face. The sound came out, clear and precise, the cluck, cluck, clucking of a hen. Turkeys, he told me, roost in tall trees. At sunup they come off the roost and begin their daily hunt for grasshoppers or acorns. When they first touch the ground, the males, the gobblers, let out a cry, a gobble, usually just one cry, and then they start their quest for food.

The game for the hunter is to listen for that first gobble, often miles away, and to answer with the cluck from the caller. It is a game of skill, to fool the gobbler, to bring him closer and closer.

Granddad liked this spot. He had hunted here for years. From here he could see up the ridge to a clearing, or, if the gobbler came along the logging trail, he had a clear view. He told me more about the gobbler, how he was ever alert, keen-eyed, sharp-hearing, a wise bird attuned to the sounds of the woods.

A person's slightest movement would be detected in a flash, a noisy deer nearby ignored. He told me how to tell a hen from a gobbler. While their crowns may look alike and their strides the same, gobblers have beards coming from the center of their chests. Longer the beard, older the bird.

"Look for the beard," Granddad said, "for it is a fat, older gobbler we want."

I watched every move my grandfather made. Finally, he poked my arm.

"Hear that?" he said.

I hadn't. Then I strained to listen and I heard my first turkey. It was way up on the ridge. Granddad stroked his caller, sounding, I thought, just like a hen. And a few moments later, an answer.

He whispered to me, "A long way off. Wait. Be still."

As I sat there the sun broke over the hills, and streamers of sun bore down upon us from around and through the trees. I felt the warmth on my face and hands. It was as if someone else had joined us. We heard the cry of crows on the ridge. "They're over the turkey. They're teasing him," he told me.

We stayed in that spot for hours, Granddad bringing the gobbler closer and closer. But by seven o'clock, nothing. No more gobbles. No answers to the caller. "We'll call it a day," he said, and we returned home.

I went hunting for wild turkeys several more times that spring, and Granddad went during the week when I was in school. He was determined to win the contest with the turkey. Obviously the turkey was just as determined. Soon spring gave way to summer and there was much to do. The summer meant my mother picked her vegetables, canned them for winter. The kitchen filled with steam and heat during the hottest months. We made a good crop of hay. I sometimes drove the tractor; sometimes I rode the wagon and stacked square bales that our helpers tossed onto the flatbed.

In no time, it seemed, summer was over, the long days shortened, and the school bus awaited me every morning at the end of the driveway. By October we had settled in for the winter, sunflowers had gone, only half stalks left.

As Thanksgiving approached, my grandfather sat closer to the warmth of the kitchen stove and his days outside were fewer and fewer. But he was determined to get a gobbler. It was, he told us, the same old bird that we had heard on my first hunt. He had called it many times since.

The week before Thanksgiving my mother made an announcement. She had saved her pennies, she said, and had just enough to buy a turkey. A dollar eighty cents, she said, would buy a fat bird and we would have a Thanksgiving meal like never before, my cousins coming from Blackstone. A dinner with pecan pie, sweet potatoes, corn cakes, green beans and okra canned from the garden—and a turkey.

I came home from school that Friday and Granddad greeted me at the door.

"Eat your supper and get to bed early," he said. "We are going to go up to our spot and get that gobbler, once and for all."

When we left the porch and headed across the field the next morning, a blanket of frost covered the ground, making it slippery. The earth crunched beneath our boots. The barrel of my shotgun was cold to the touch, and we blew ghosts with our breath as we approached Cedar Run.

When we reached the bank, a ledge of ice looking like lace clung to the sides of the creek, and we tried to walk quietly to the logging trail and to the fallen tree. It was bitter cold in the dark. We sat on the wet ground, the dampness seeping into my skin, making me even colder. And we waited and waited. Finally the first light, then sunup, then the quick breeze that comes up with the sun, a rustling of leaves, birds moving about the hackberry trees, seeking breakfast, a few stray squirrels, but mostly quiet. I remember thinking that we were the only people awake on the face of the earth.

My grandfather sat there, his back to the log, his hands jammed into his pockets, his caller next to him on the ground, his shotgun resting against the log. Then a gobble. I heard it on the first call. It was close, I thought. We looked at each other. My grandfather picked up his caller, struck it twice, making little quiet clucks, and there was an immediate response. Our Thanksgiving Day turkey was there for sure.

Over the next hour there was an exchange of voices: the gobbler's and my grandfather's. The gobbler was coming to us.

My grandfather whispered, "Cock your gun. You're going to get that bird."

I was excited beyond words.

Minutes later there was a gobbler so clear, so close that it frightened me. On the logging trail just below us, in the clear, the wily bird stood facing us. He was a monstrous bird. Big, barrel-chested, tall, looking first one way then another. He had been fooled.

As I watched him move slowly toward us, I could see myself at the dinner table, my grandfather carving the turkey, my mother telling one and all how I had put the turkey on our dinner table. I thought of the long year, and how I wanted to hug my mother and tell her she could save her pennies for Christmas or whatever else she wanted.

Then I saw the beard. It was protruding from his breast so long that it dragged the ground. I thought I saw wisps of gray adding to its age, gray amongst the long strands of black. I lifted my gun and I had dead aim. I would fire. One shot. That was all I needed. Suddenly my grandfather jumped to his feet, and, in the confusion that followed, the turkey flew at us and over us, breaking dried limbs from trees with his wings, crying out in fright. He disappeared over the ridge. Lost.

I turned to my grandfather. "I had him, Granddad!" I cried. "I had him." Before I finished the sentence he had started walking toward home. "Granddad," I said. But he did not listen. Stooped though he was, he walked determinedly toward home.

As we crossed Cedar Run, our boots chipping away at the ice along the banks, I faced him again. He put his arm across my shoulder.

"The beard," he said. "Did you see the beard? Old bird. He's been in these woods as long, as long..."

As long as you, I thought.

We had a store-bought turkey that Thanksgiving. Granddad sat at the head of the table, and we held hands as he said a prayer. We had a glorious time. I can remember to this day the smell of that turkey in the oven, the taste of the pecan pie, and the serene look on Granddad's face.